THIS BOOK BELONGS TO:

ISBN 978-1-4521-2893-1

Manufactured in China.

Illustrations by Micah Player.
Text by Naomi Kirsten.
Design by Anne Kenady.
Typeset in Century Schoolbook.

10 9 8 7 6 5 4 3 2 1

Chronicle Books LLC
680 Second Street
San Francisco, CA 94107

Chronicle Books—we see things differently.
Become part of our community at www.chroniclekids.com.

lately lily
BOOK of FUN

DOODLE & DISCOVER YOUR WORLD!

chronicle books · san francisco

DRAW A MEMORY from one of your favorite vacations. Add as many details as possible!

Zeborah has just made a new friend in **PARIS**.
Draw what they are about to do next!

Imagine that this is your very own **PLANE!**
Draw designs all over it!

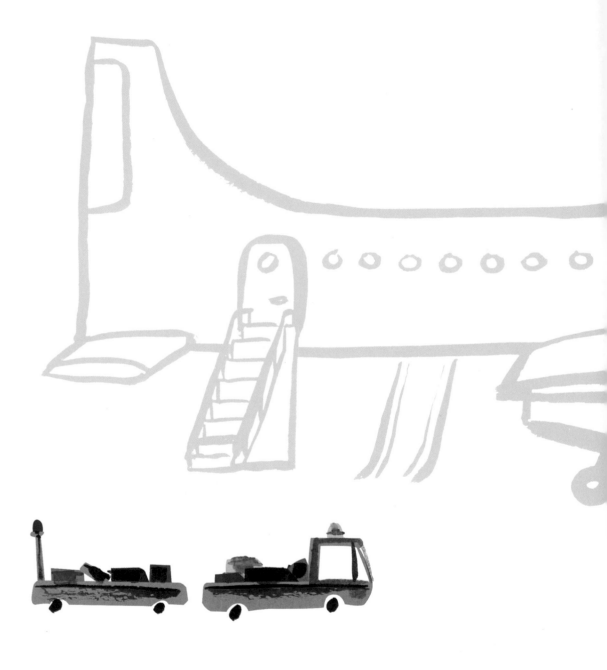

DESIGN YOUR SUITCASE! Sometimes it's hard to spot your suitcase in baggage claim, so design a suitcase that's sure to stand out!

I've just landed in . . . **PARIS!** One of my favorite things about this city is the food. Color in some of my favorite treats, and then learn their names!

QUICHE

TARTE TATIN

MACARON

MADELEINES

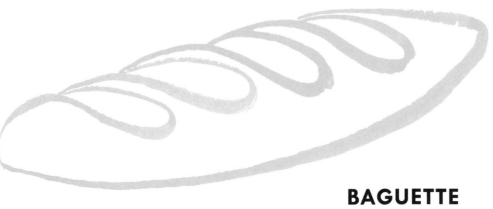

BAGUETTE

I love collecting **PASSPORT STAMPS** when I travel.
Draw some stamps in your passport here!

I can't stop taking pictures of **ZEBORAH!** Draw the snaps I've taken of him in all of the frames!

Take an **AIRPLANE RIDE** with me! Draw yourself
in an airplane window, and anyone else
you'd like to travel with!

When I visit my friend Klara in Sweden, we always play music together. Draw the other members of our band. I hope one of them is **YOU!**

Taste the flavors of the world! That's what I like to do.
Draw as many **ICE-CREAM SCOOPS** as you can.

Help me pack for a **BEACH VACATION!** Draw what I'll need for this trip in my suitcase. Use my list as a guide.

BATHING SUIT
BEACH BLANKET
GOGGLES
SHORTS
T-SHIRTS

PICNICS ARE THE BEST!
Draw the treats Zeborah and I are about to eat.

Z is for **ZEBORAH!**
Color in the all of the Zs on these pages.

TIME TO TAKE A HIKE! Color in the mountains around me, and draw some forest creatures, too.

I haven't seen my friend Yun Li in so long! She has thrown a welcome party for me! **COLOR** in the balloons, **DRAW** the food, and **DECORATE** the space!

Travelling by airplane gives me the chance to look (and look and look) out the window. **DRAW WHAT I SEE!**

One of my favorite things to do at the beach is to look for **SEASHELLS**. Check out some of the shells I found— then color them in!

When I travel, I like to people watch. I also like to dog watch. **COLOR IN THE DOGS** I've seen on my travels.

DACHSHUND

BEAGLE

YORKSHIRE
TERRIER

BULLDOG

Just a quiet night, harmonizing with Zeborah . . .
AND YOU! Draw yourself at our campsite, and
then color in (and count!) all of the stars!

I like to think about this a lot! If you could bring only **FIVE THINGS** to keep you busy on a deserted island, what would they be? Draw them on the island.

WORD GAME! Circle the first letter in each word below, and then write each first letter in the spaces below.

LAKE
ISLAND
LIGHTHOUSE
YURT

___ ___ ___ ___

Color in the word you wrote here!

Yup, I can be a candy collector, sampling the sweet treats that a city has to offer. **NO TWO CHOCOLATES ARE ALIKE!** Fill up my box of treats by drawing chocolates from Paris.

There are many ways to get around busy cities
without a car. **DRAW ZEBORAH** zipping
around on his many different rides!

FRUIT-TASTIC! The world is full of amazing fruits. Check out some of the ones I've discovered on my travels, and color the others in!

GRAPES

DURIAN

CHERIMOYA

ORANGE

CARAMBOLA (STAR FRUIT)

LEMON

**PITAYA
(DRAGON FRUIT)**

COCONUT

POMEGRANATE

BANANA

DESERT DISCOVERIES . . . there's nothing like exploring by camel! Draw what I am seeing on and in the sand!

SAFARI SNAPSHOTS! Draw what I saw while on safari.
What kinds of animals did I see?

Zeborah and I are exploring a **CAVE!**
Draw what we discover there.

First stop after the airport: the hotel! This hotel is one of my favorites. **COLOR IN THE BUILDINGS** of the neighborhood, and draw more of your own!

Whenever I'm in New York City, I love going to the symphony. **DRAW SOME OF YOUR FAVORITE INSTRUMENTS.** Here is one of mine—the cello. What are some of yours?

I need to pack for a **CAMPING TRIP** in the mountains.
Use my list to draw all I need to have a fantastic time!

HAT
JACKET
TROUSERS
HIKING BOOTS
TENT

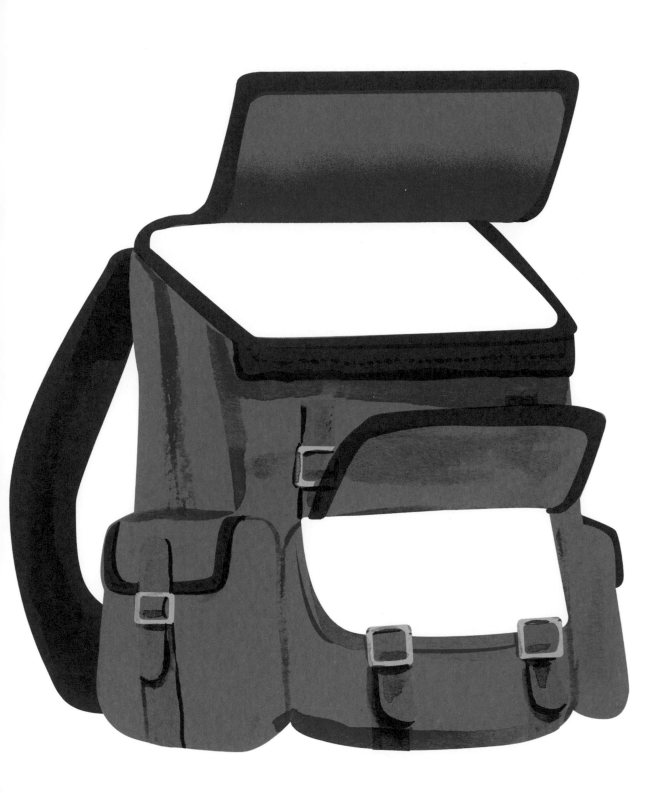

Travelling during the fall means trees with leaves in so many colors. Draw **RED, YELLOW, AND ORANGE** leaves on all of the trees.

People celebrate different holidays during the winter months. What do you **CELEBRATE** each year? Draw that celebration here, and draw me celebrating with you!

One of Zeborah's favorite treats in Amsterdam is the **GIANT PANCAKE.** He likes to top his pancake with apples, bananas, chocolate, and even marshmallows! Draw your your favorite toppings on this pancake.

WORD GAME! Circle the first letter in each word below, and then write each first letter in the spaces below.

ZOO

ELEPHANT

BISTRO

OCEAN

RAFT

AIRPLANE

HOTEL

___ ___ ___ ___ ___ ___ ___

Color in the word you wrote here!

Lunchtime . . . **ON THE BEACH!** Color in some of my favorite beach eats, and then draw some of your own.

The city of Lisbon in Portugal is known for its many **COLORFUL** and **DETAILED** tiles. Draw your own design on this blank tile!

Tee-time, beach-style, and by "tee" I mean "shirt."
Help me design a **BEACH-THEMED** T-shirt!

No matter where he goes, Zeborah always packs a few of his **FAVORITE THINGS** in his suitcase, Blue Bell. What do you think Zeborah brings on every trip? Draw them in his Blue Bell!

Up, up, up, and away I go! When you travel by hot air balloon, **THE VIEW** is out of control! I am floating above your neighborhood right now. Draw what I see!

L is for **LILY!** Color in the L, and then draw other L words on these pages.

OFF TO . . . YOU CHOOSE!
Draw the busy scene around me. I've already started to sketch it. Thank you for helping me to finish it!

Whenever I travel, I write **EVERYTHING** down in my notebook. Use these two notebook pages to write about or draw your day.

One of the best things about travel is eating new **FOOD.** Place a checkmark beside what you'd like to try on your next trip!

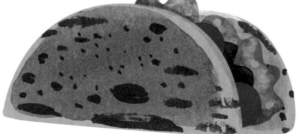

Zeborah likes it when we have a few extra hours just to run around and see everything. Draw us enjoying one of the best parts of the Singapore airport—the **BUTTERFLY GARDEN!** Draw all of the butterflies flying around us!

Zeborah is a HUGE *soccer* fan when he's in the United States. When he's most everywhere else, he's a HUGE *football* fan! Every four years, one country hosts the biggest tournament in the world, the World Cup. Draw Zeborah scoring the **WINNING GOAL!**

Rain or shine, it's all about making the most of the
weather when I travel. Draw some weather
(**RAIN, SLEET, SNOW, OR HAIL**) all around me.
And, see—I'm still smiling!

Tee-time, city-style, and by "tee" I mean "shirt."
Help me design a **CITY-THEMED** T-shirt!

If Zeborah could do **ANYTHING** on his trip to a big city, what would he do? Draw some photos of Zeborah and me enjoying the day!

Zeborah loves going to toy museums.
Draw some of the **TOYS** he is looking at right now!

It's cherry blossom season! Every spring, thousands of tourists flock to cities all over Japan to see the blooming cherry trees. Zeborah and I found a prime spot beneath one of the biggest trees in Kyoto. Draw yourself with us, and **DRAW MORE TREES!**

Discovering other countries' flags is one of my favorite things about travel. **DRAW THE FLAG** of the country where you live, and then draw the flag for your very own imaginary country!

My country's flag.

My own flag.

That's me **HANG GLIDING!** Draw the other things in the air flying along with me!

Travelling by train gives me the chance to look (and look and look) out the window. **DRAW WHAT I SEE!**

Help me pack for a **SKI TRIP!** Draw what I'll need for this trip in my suitcase. Use my list as a guide.

WOOL HAT
JACKET
TROUSERS
LONG-SLEEVE SHIRT
SOCKS
BOOTS
SKIS or
SNOWBOARD

Sometimes I travel to discover amazing sights . . . in the sky! Here I am in Abisko, Sweden, ready to view the aurora borealis—**THE NORTHERN LIGHTS!** Draw swirling colors of green, red, and yellow above my head!

When I'm in London, I love to have tea. Draw the **TEA PARTY** I'm having with Zeborah and you!

AHOY! I'm on a whale-watching trip! Color the whale beneath the sea, and draw any other sea creatures in sight!

SEA DANCER

IT'S A WINTER WONDERLAND! I am all bundled up in snowy New York City. Draw the snowflakes that are falling all around me, and some skyscrapers, too.

Exploring **LIBRARIES** in different cities is one of my favorite things to do while travelling! Draw a library with books everywhere.

Zeborah and I are having a blast in the **SNOW!**
Draw the snowman (or snow woman) we just made!

Zeborah and I have just built the
BIGGEST SAND CASTLE EVER. Draw it!

The tallest mountain in the world is Mount Everest in the Himalayas. Draw **YOU AND ME** at the very top. We made it!

DRESS UP ZEBORAH! What should he wear on his different trips? Color in his outfits.

Tee-time, desert-style, and by "tee" I mean "shirt."
Help me design a **DESERT-THEMED** T-shirt!

SURPRISES UNDER THE SEA! I love to snorkel. Draw the different fish and ocean animals around me!

SHHHH! I love secret parks. Many cities in Europe have tucked-away parks that I stumble upon when I walk around the city. Draw the details of the park around me. This one's in Paris.

SURF'S UP! I'm learning to surf.
Draw Zeborah and me on our surfboards!

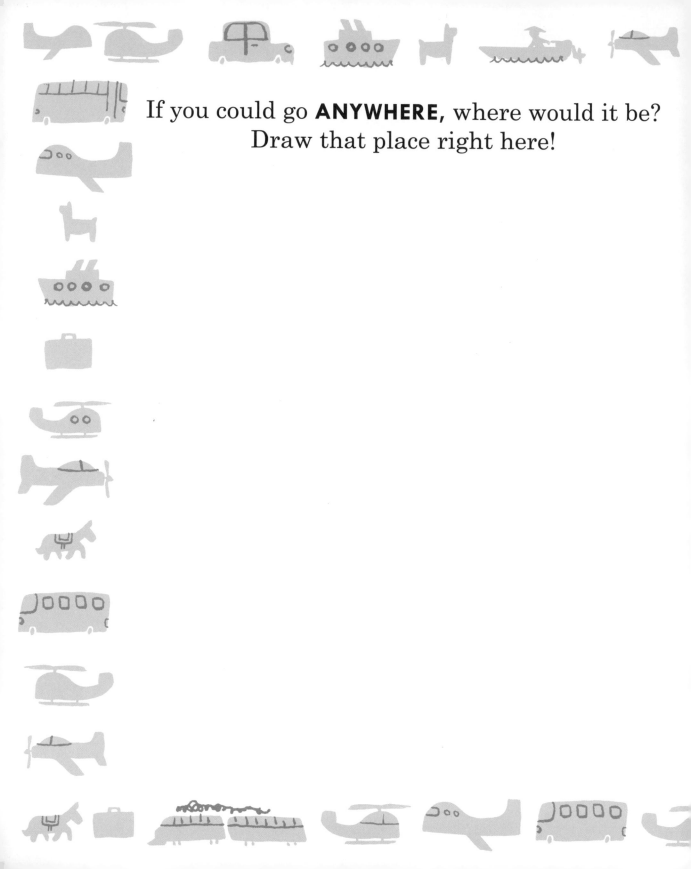

If you could go **ANYWHERE**, where would it be?
Draw that place right here!

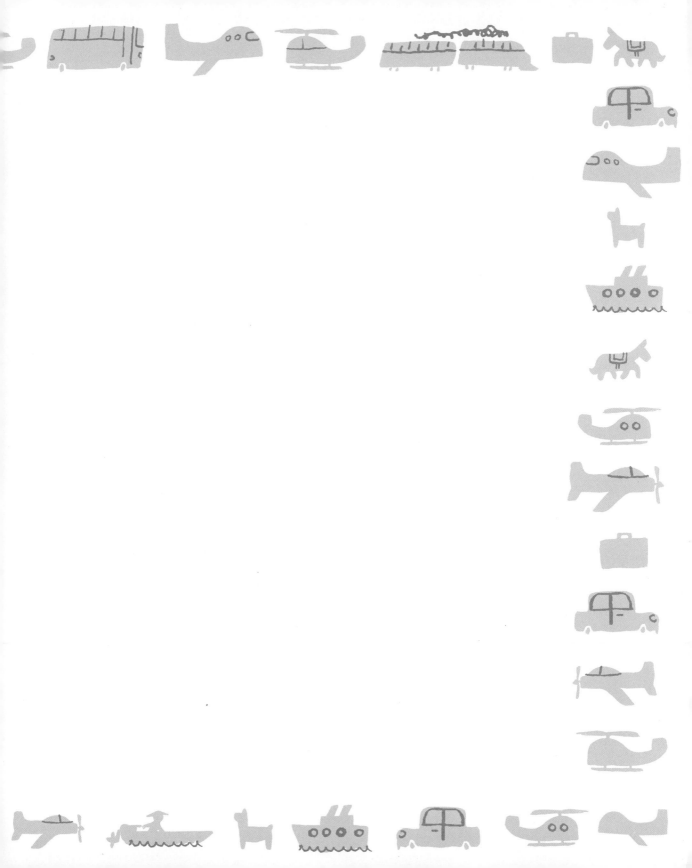

I hope you've had as much fun with this book as I have!
Remember: The **WORLD** is yours to explore!
Happy travelling, no matter where you go!

until
next time!
♡ lily